MW00879271

ISBN: 9781087868295

S.B. Publishing

Kira.Bradwell@aol.com

It's our first day of camp, I don't know what
we should wear, hmm yeah my favorite
T-shirt and sneakers, yeah, yeah, that will do,
said Kammie and me.

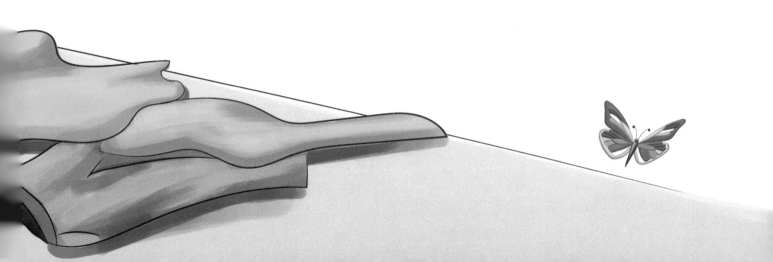

Well, we made it Kammie! What should we do first? I don't know, replied Kammie, I just hope they see me and not you this time, so please try to stay still, focused, remain calm and remember it's ok to take a break, you know...

Oh, my! I'm so excited Kammie, I hope we get picked next to play kick ball! Wait, wait, wait I think I heard mom telling the camp counselor Dorsey when she dropped us off this morning, that we may drift off and our balance is a little off, when we play, ugh...I wonder does everyone know, Kammie replied sadly.

Please, pick, me, please pick me
Kammie, chanted quietly, to herself.

Oh, my goodness it's happening again, Kammie thought
to herself, I'm getting anxious; nobody's going to pick me.
I wonder if anyone notices that my thoughts are starting
to get scrabbled up like eggs.

Please, please, please don't scream don't run away, they'll just laugh at us and won't pick us, Kammie said to herself, when just as she was about to scream, two kids yelled we want Kammie on our team. Kammie couldn't believe it she ran as fast as she could to join the group.

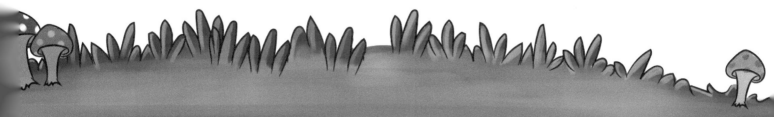

Kammie was relieved she had the best first day of camp ever and she made two new friends Tanner and Leslie. She even scored the winning kick! When, all the kids were packing up to leave, Kammie and I thought to ourselves why would they ever pick us? We, talk to ourselves and let's face it one of us really can't be seen, so I told Kammie she should ask Tanner and Leslie why they picked us, so......here it goes!

Hey, hey, Kammie said with excitement why did you and Leslie picked us, oops! I meant me to play on your kick ball team? Hope, they didn't pick us because of our difference or because the teacher asked them to, thought Kammie to herself. Tanner replied, with excitement he hardly could stay still... it was a no, brainer we thought if we picked you Kammie we'd get two friends out of one! They loved Kammie and Me afterall!

Discussion Questions

How do you think Kammie felt at the beginning of the story and why?

Has there ever been a time you've felt like Kammie?

What are some ways that we can make our friends that may be different feel better about themselves?

Activity

Draw a picture of a time you helped a family member or a friend.

Activity
Draw how helping them, made you feel.

"Children with Autism are Colorful-They are Often Very Beautiful and, Like a Butterfly, They Stand Out."

Adele Devine

CPSIA information can be obtained
at www.ICGtesting.com
Printed in the USA
BVHW021727070521
606754BV00009BA/312